# A Serenade of Mermaids

# A Serenade of Mermaids

## Mermaid Tales from Around the World

COLLECTED, RETOLD, & ANNOTATED BY
*Shirley Climo*

ILLUSTRATED BY
*Lisa Falkenstern*

HarperTrophy®
*A Division of HarperCollinsPublishers*

# A Serenade of Mermaids

*For Blanche,*
*our first mermaid*

Harper Trophy® is a registered trademark
of HarperCollins Publishers Inc.

Originally published in 1997 as a picture book,
with illustrations by Jean and Mou-sien Tseng

A Serenade of Mermaids: Mermaid Tales from Around the World
Text copyright © 1997 by Shirley Climo
Illustrations copyright © 1999 by Linda Falkenstern

Library of Congress Cataloging-in-Publication Data
Climo, Shirley.
    [a treasury of mermaids]
    Serenade of mermaids / by Shirley Climo ; illustrated by Lisa
Falkenstern.
        p.    cm.
    Contents: Mrs. Fitzgerald the Merrow (Ireland) — The legend
of Aymee and the mermaid (Alaska) — Odysseus and the Sirens
(Greece) — Hansi and the nix (Switzerland) — And then the merman
laughed (Iceland) — The listening ear (Japan) — The sea witch and
the sea princess (Hebrides Islands, Scotland) — Pania of the reef
(New Zealand) — Notes on the stories.
    ISBN 0-06-442103-1 (pbk.)
    1. Mermaids—Folklore.   2. Tales.   [1. Mermaids—Folklore.
2. Folklore.]
I. Falkenstern, Lisa, ill.   II. Title.
PZ8.1.C592Se   1999                                        98-44272
398.21—dc21                                                    CIP
                                                              AC

Typography by Alison Donalty
2   3   4   5   6   7   8   9   10
❖
Newly Illustrated Harper Trophy Edition, 1999

Visit us on the World Wide Web!
http://www.harperchildrens.com

# Contents

watched the green and violet northern lights dance above her head. When a blizzard blew, she huddled inside her house and listened to the singsong of the wind. This was her dream-

# Introduction

In medieval England *mermaid* was spelled *mere-mayde*. *Mayde* meant "maiden." A *mere* could be a sea, a lake, or even just a swampy place. A mermaid is simply a water woman, good or bad. She drifts beneath the ocean waves, lies unseen in river rushes, and sleeps in shaded ponds. A streak of rainbow glinting in a puddle might mean a mermaid is there. Even so, catching one of these magical beings isn't easy. A mermaid can disappear without a trace, evaporating like a drop of water on a summer day.

All water holds hidden magic. Without it there can be no life on earth. But too much of it washes life away, in tidal waves and typhoons, in floods and hurricanes. Some of our oldest stories are "water warnings" that caution of its dangers. That's why we're told of terrifying mer-monsters as well as enchanting mermaids, and why tales about these mysterious underwater creatures don't always end happily ever after.

Our best-known mermaid folktales come from Europe, where they've been recorded for thousands of years. Now stories about other merpeople, from other regions of the world, are becoming more familiar. Many of these tales are also very old but have not been written down until recently. Some of them are in this book.

So if you'd like to meet a mermaid, you'll find one waiting for you here.

# Mrs. Fitzgerald the Merrow

Once mermaids swam in all the salty seas, as common as sardines. But unlike fish in a can, all mermaids aren't alike. Although most are young and beautiful, some comb golden locks while others have hair as green as sea grass or as dark as the midnight sea.

Mermaids come in different sizes, too. In Malaysia they tell of one so small, she slept in a clamshell. A Celtic account, written in A.D. 887, reported a mermaid who measured one hundred and sixty feet from head to tail and had fingers seven feet long. That was a whale of a lady!

Usually mermaids have fishtails, but some have legs instead. A few have legs *and* tails. A mermaid with legs—or one who keeps her tail hidden—looks like an ordinary girl. Only sharp eyes can spy the ducklike webs between her toes or fingers.

In British stories a mermaid is often recognized by the comb or mirror she holds in her hand. In Germany it's the hem of her apron that gives her away. If it's dripping wet, she's sure to be a mermaid.

An Irish mermaid, called a *merrow*, is known by the peaked red hat she wears. With it upon her head, the merrow can breathe underwater. But should she lose her hat, then that's a different story. . . .

$\mathcal{E}$arly one morning, as the sun began to color the ocean blue, Dick Fitzgerald stood on the Dingle shore and stared out to sea. He was looking at nothing in particular when he chanced to glimpse something green perched upon a rock.

"Bless me!" said Dick, squinting. "Can it be a green seal?"

That deserved a closer look, so Dick took off his boots, rolled his trousers to his knees, and slipped and slid across the mossy rocks until he'd gotten near to the creature.

"Bless me twice over!" Dick exclaimed softly. For now he could see that it was not a seal at all but a girl combing seaweed from her long, green hair. She was a mermaid, he was certain, for she'd a bit of a tail and there was a little red hat beside her on the rock. "And a magical cap it is," whispered Dick, "so I'll just take it for safekeeping."

He snatched the hat and stuffed it into his

pocket. The mermaid did not see him, for her back was to him. But when Dick's foot slipped, splashing into the water, she heard him.

Startled, the mermaid turned around. A corner of her hat peeped from Dick's pocket. "Oh! Oh! Oh!" she wailed, and tears spilled from her eyes.

Dick guessed why she was crying, but he was not about to hand over her magic hat until he saw what luck might come of it. He pulled a handkerchief from his other pocket instead. "Try this," he suggested.

The mermaid took it and blew her nose. "Man," she asked in a trembly voice, "are you going to eat me?"

"Eat you?" cried Dick. "I never! You've been listening to fish tales."

"Man," the mermaid said again, "if you'll not eat me, what will you do with me?"

"Whatever will I do with you?" he echoed, for he'd not really thought about that. He studied the mermaid from the top of her green head to her little webbed toes. She was a lovely lass, that was the truth, and he was lonely. And so he said, "I suppose I might marry you."

Now the mermaid studied Dick Fitzgerald. He had a nice smile and curly black hair and was far handsomer than any merman. "I suppose I might marry you, too," she agreed.

Dick took her hand to lead her up the path to his house, but the mermaid pulled away. "Wait!" she said, and bent to whisper into the sea. Her words spread out from the shore in ripples.

"Is it the salt water you're speaking to?" wondered Dick.

"I'm telling my father not to wait breakfast," the mermaid replied.

"And who is your father?"

"To be sure, he's King of the Waves."

"That makes you a princess!" he cried. "And makes Dick Fitzgerald the luckiest man in Dingle!"

"Who's he?" asked the mermaid, looking around for another.

"He's me," Dick answered. "And when we're

wed, you'll be Mrs. Fitzgerald."

"Mrs. Fitzgerald the Merrow," said she, trying it out on her tongue. "It does have a nice ring to it."

And so they were married, and Dick carried the newly named Mrs. Fitzgerald over the threshold into his house. While she was exclaiming over the pots and pans and feather pillows, he tucked her little red hat into a cubbyhole in the fireplace chimney and covered it with an old, torn fishing net. Now that he had met his merrow, he'd not chance losing her.

Mrs. Fitzgerald enjoyed playing house. She learned how to sew, although she always poked her finger with the needle. She learned to brew a pot of tea and to make oat porridge, although she often scorched it. But when it came to frying a fish, the mermaid shuddered and said, "I will not cook one of the family!"

Some things Mrs. Fitzgerald could not or would not learn. She thought housecleaning was silly and kept crabs as pets in her washtub. She didn't care a tiddly-tot for money, either, and every time she shopped, she lost a few pence.

"If coins were as pretty as seashells, I'd keep count," she explained.

Dick just wagged his head and grumbled, "Mrs. Fitzgerald, whatever will I do with you?"

When he said that, as he did quite often, the mermaid kissed him and promised to do better.

The two of them were happy, all the same. They were even happier when they had three fine children, two boys and a girl. The mermaid hung starfish over their cradles and sang the three to sleep with sea chanties, so she was disappointed when they didn't take to water. It was even a struggle to get them into a bathtub on Saturday nights.

The children grew up, as even a mermaid's will do, and Mr. and Mrs. Fitzgerald were alone again. Her green hair had turned to gray, and they looked like ordinary old folks. They acted like them too. Mrs. Fitzgerald seldom mentioned the ocean anymore, and Dick seldom needed to ask, "Whatever will I do with you?"

One day Dick had to travel to Tralee. "You've half a holiday," he told his wife, "for I'll not be home till teatime."

Mrs. Fitzgerald waved him off and went inside. "I'll surprise Dick and tidy up a bit," she said.

At first she couldn't recall where she kept her broom and mop and bucket, for it had been an age and a day since she'd cleaned. But once she found them, she soon had the house swept and scrubbed. She was quite pleased with herself until she saw sticky cobwebs dangling from the rafters.

"Oh, fishhooks!" cried Mrs. Fitzgerald, annoyed.

She swung her broom about, sending spiders flying. One swish of the broom chanced too close to the fireplace chimney and snagged an old fishing net. The net fell to the floor and with it came a red hat.

"I've seen this wee cap," said Mrs. Fitzgerald, "perhaps in a dream." She shook off the dust. "I might just try it on."

The moment the hat touched her head, her hair turned green again. She looked as she had on the morning she'd first met Dick Fitzgerald. Her head flooded with sea memories of her father the king, her mother the queen, and all of her dozens of sisters and brothers.

"I'm glad I told them I'd be late for breakfast," she cried as she ran out the door.

The ocean was calm and smooth, and the merrow — for she was fully one again — thought she heard soft, sweet songs inviting her into the water. "I'll only pay a small visit," she promised herself, "and then I'll be back." Holding the red hat tight to her head, she plunged into the waves.

When Dick Fitzgerald came home, he found the front door open wide and the fishing net heaped on the floor. He knew what must have happened and where his wife must be. He hurried down to the shore.

At the water's edge, Dick cupped his hands and shouted, "Come home, Mrs. Fitzgerald! Come home! Whatever will I do without you?"

Then he sat down on the sand and stared at the sea, looking for something in particular. And there Dick Fitzgerald may sit yet, even to this day.

# The Legend of Aymee
# and the Mermaid

Mermaids are world travelers.

Christopher Columbus claimed to see mermaids bobbing about in the waves as he sailed across the Atlantic.

Norse fishermen brought with them to Iceland and Greenland their belief in sea trolls, and they imagined an ocean swimming with merfolk.

When Africans came to the New World, stories of water spirits came too. Among the islands of the Caribbean a mermaid is called Mama Alo, just as she was in the Old World.

Soon after these newcomers arrived, they discovered that Native Americans had their own water people, both good and bad.

Wanagemeswak, the helpful hatchet-faced spirits of the Penobscot, burrow in riverbanks and pools.

Salt Woman, said to live at the bottom of the Salt Sea, gave the gift of salt to the Zuni people.

The Illinois Indians frightened settlers with tales of vicious men-fish skulking in the muddy Mississippi, while the Chiriquí of Panama fear a river god who is half man, half alligator.

Eskimos tell about Sedna, the fierce sea goddess who, with her single eye, oversees everything in the ocean. They also speak of a gentler water woman, a true mermaid, called a *nuyaqpalik*.

$\mathcal{N}$ear the Arctic Circle, at the tip of a thumb-shape peninsula that juts into the Chukchi Sea, is the Inupiat village of Kotzebue. Here, on the inlet's pebbly shore, stood the small sod house of a young woman named Aymee.

Aymee had lived in the Arctic for all her short life. She loved the long, shining days of summer, when the sun never left the sky to rest in the sea. But she did not dislike the months of darkness. Then, if the sky was clear, she watched the green and violet northern lights dance above her head. When a blizzard blew, she huddled inside her house and listened to the singsong of the wind. This was her dreaming time.

One year was different from any Aymee could remember. By midsummer, although the days were warm, flocks of ptarmigans had flown away, leaving empty nests behind. When autumn came, only a few dusty-brown hares remained to play hide-and-seek among the clumps of tundra grass. Caribou were scarce, and hardly any salmon swam up the rivers. The villagers ate what tomcod they could catch, and nothing was dried for the stormy days ahead.

"A bad summer means a worse winter," warned the village elders. "Our stomachs will grumble with hunger."

On a chilly fall day, when frozen lichen crunched beneath her boots, Aymee went looking for any crowberries that might still cling to the low bushes near the shore. She had gathered only two or three handfuls when she was startled by a loud splash. Aymee hurried to the water's edge, but the inlet was as still and smooth as a looking glass.

"Why does no one fish here?" she asked aloud. "Men catch salmon in the river and hunt walrus in the ocean."

Aymee stared at the water. If a fish had jumped before, she did not see one now. "Nothing will be lost by putting out a net," she declared.

Aymee dragged a kayak to the shore and pulled out a willow-bark net. She anchored the net with a rock before stretching it out in the water. The net was large and awkward, and only the floats kept it from sinking.

Then she drifted silently in the kayak, waiting. She waited throughout the afternoon, making a scanty supper of the crowberries, but nothing disturbed the water.

"I'd find more fish in a puddle," she said at last, and paddled back to her house by the shore.

She was asleep, dreaming of fat fish sputtering over a fire, when a noise awakened her. Aymee lay still beneath her rabbit-skin cover, listening. Far away, *amaguq,* the wolf, wailed. Close by, *ukpik,* the owl, hooted. And then . . .

"Yi-i-i-i!"

Aymee shivered. No ordinary animal made such a sound. She pulled on her parka and went out the door flap. The new day had scarcely begun, for the sky was still a yellow-green. The cry came again, rising from the bay, and Aymee

could see the water churning. The skin rope that held her net strained at its mooring, and the net itself was heaving as if it were caught in a whirlpool.

Aymee had just pushed her kayak from shore when a huge wave almost swamped it. First a fishtail, then a head thrust from the water. The tail was covered with silvery scales, but the head had black hair like Aymee's own.

"A *nuyaqpalik!*" whispered Aymee. "A mermaid!"

The mermaid's long hair was tangled in the willow-bark net. Again and again she twisted about, trying to free herself.

When the mermaid saw Aymee, she spit a mouthful of water and bared her teeth. "Yi! Yi!" she shrieked, and this time her cry was in anger.

"I will help you if I can," said Aymee. She chose brave words, but her voice shook. Cautiously, she paddled nearer.

As the kayak approached, the mermaid gave

up her thrashing and sank from sight in the bay. Aymee leaned over the side of the boat to look for her. Suddenly two arms reached up and tried to overturn the kayak into the icy bay.

"Stop!" shouted Aymee, pushing the mermaid away with her paddle. "If you drown *me*, who will save you?"

Fingernails scraped the side of the boat as the *nuyaqpalik* slowly loosened her hold.

"You must be quiet if I am to untangle your hair."

The mermaid stared silently at Aymee, neither snarling nor smiling. Slowly Aymee reached for the net and began to separate the long hair from the mesh, strand by strand. As she worked, she talked. She talked to soothe the sea maiden, as well as to quiet her own thumping heart. "I am a woman, just as you."

The mermaid gasped as Aymee tugged her hair, but she did not cry out.

"But you are the loveliest woman I have ever seen," added Aymee, and she meant it.

This sea-creature-with-a-tail was more beautiful than any land maiden. "No wonder men are said to fall in love with the *nuyaqpalik*."

The mermaid's brown eyes gleamed. She seemed to understand.

"The men of my village have not caught many caribou," Aymee continued, "nor scarcely any fish." She combed the thick hair with her fingers. "That was why I set this net. Not to trap you, but to trap whitefish."

The mermaid was still, listening, not making a ripple. Aymee told legends of Kotzebue, about her people. She told the mermaid her dreams, as well.

"That is the end of my story," she said at last. "And it may be the end for others, too. Without food for the winter, many in Kotzebue will starve."

The mermaid blinked, and Aymee thought she saw tears. Perhaps that was because Aymee had had to yank to loosen the last handful of hair.

"There!" said Aymee. "See if you can pull free."

The mermaid plunged into the bay, shaking

off the net, and leaped up again. She rolled over and over in the water, frolicking like a seal pup. Aymee laughed to see her. Then she looked up at the sun. She had spent the whole day untangling the mermaid's hair.

"It is late," she said to the mermaid, "and now I must reset my net for fish. Take care you are not trapped again."

The mermaid reached out and touched Aymee's hand. Then, with a slap of her tail, she vanished in the water.

The very next morning the small bay was swarming with whitefish. Aymee's net was so full, it sank to the bottom. Of course, when she shared her fish with the villagers, she had to share the secret of the mermaid, too. Soon many nets floated in the bay, and enough whitefish were caught to feed Kotzebue throughout the winter.

Although every autumn thereafter whitefish swarmed into the bay, the *nuyaqpalik* never returned. Only Aymee saw her again. She met her mermaid again each winter, in her dreaming time.

# Odysseus and the Sirens

Strange and supernatural beings have made their homes in the water for thousands of years.

People in ancient Babylonia believed that Cannes, a man-fish, had brought them the gift of wisdom from the depths of the Persian Gulf.

Old tales from India describe a fish-god named Varuna. His breath is the wind that swells the sails of ships.

According to early Greeks, the ocean flows around the earth like a great river. The guardian of this wide stream of salt water was a Titan named Oceanus. His three thousand daughters—the Oceanids—were said to be the dancing waves. Nereids, fifty nymphs, inhabited the inland seas, while a Naiad, another female spirit, might be found in waterfalls and lakes. Most powerful of all the water dwellers was the god Poseidon. As ruler of the sea, whatever happened in or on the water was up to him.

Among the oldest recorded mermaid tales is the story of the Sirens. These were beautiful but brutal nymphs who drifted in the treacherous waters that surrounded their peaceful islet. With enchanting songs they lured Greek sailors to certain death.

Sirens gave their name to the warning wails of police and fire vehicles. Today, these cries signal "Danger!" just as they did when a Greek named Odysseus first heard the Sirens calling long ago.

*I*n ancient Greece, so poets said, there once lived a man named Odysseus. He was king of the island of Ithaca and fought with great courage in the Trojan War. When those battles ended, Odysseus declared, "At last I can go home."

The king prepared to return to Ithaca. He gathered a fleet of twelve war galleys. Each galley was supplied with food and water and manned by forty oarsmen. But Odysseus forgot to give thanks to the gods for helping the Greeks to victory. This neglect angered all the gods, but it was Poseidon, ruler of the sea, who determined to teach Odysseus a lesson.

"Some surprises will await bold Odysseus on this voyage," vowed that god.

The fleet had scarcely lifted anchor before fearful things began to happen. With violent storms Poseidon blew the ships far off course. Some sank, battered by winds and swamped by waves, and many men drowned. One misadventure followed another until only one galley and a handful of sailors remained. A desperate Odysseus sought safety on the Isle of Dawn.

The island belonged to an enchantress named Circe. As soon as the Greeks beached their boat on the sands, she bewitched them. Circe turned the sailors into snuffling, snorting pigs. Although Odysseus himself resisted her spells, much time passed before he could persuade Circe to change his men back to their human forms.

"Now we can set sail again," said Odysseus, "knowing we have left the worst behind."

"Not so," cautioned Circe. "Ahead lies the Island of the Sirens. Those water nymphs wait to snare unwary sailors with their songs. Their music drives men wild. Those who listen cast themselves into the ocean and suffer a frightful end."

The sailors heard Circe's warning and began to mutter among themselves.

"I hear that Sirens thirst for human blood," one declared.

"Our swords and shields will be useless against them," said another.

"Let us stay here," a third suggested. "Far better to live as pigs than to die at the hands of the Sirens."

"Those are the words of cowards," Odysseus told them, scornful. "Are you not true Greeks, brave and battle tested?"

The men dropped their eyes, unable to answer their leader's challenge. It was Circe who broke the silence.

"Perhaps there is a way for your men to escape the Sirens," she offered. "Have you beeswax among your provisions, good king?"

"We have a portion aboard to aid in the mending of sails," he replied.

"Let it serve a more important purpose," Circe said. "Stopper everyone's ears with wax. Those who do not hear the Sirens may journey safely past them."

"Clever Circe!" Odysseus exclaimed. "The goddess of wisdom herself could not give better advice."

The next day, as dawn colored the sky, Odysseus ordered the sailors to launch the galley. The oarsmen took their places on the rowing benches, and the ship once again put out to sea.

At midday, Odysseus sighted a gray granite ledge rising abruptly from the ocean. The flat rock had neither grass nor trees, but was strewn with seaweed and dotted with patches of white as dazzling as polished marble. In the frothy water below, figures splashed and dived like dolphins. But these looked to be sea dwellers of another sort.

"We approach the Sirens!" shouted Odysseus. "Rest oars!"

As the galley drifted closer to the island, Odysseus took a ball of beeswax from the ship's supplies and kneaded it until it was soft. He gave two pebble-size pieces to each man.

"Plug your ears well," he told them, "so that you are deaf to the singing of the Sirens."

"No wax remains for you!" an oarsman objected.

"I need none. I will watch and listen until we have left all danger behind us."

"What if the Sirens lure *you* overboard?" one asked. "Without our king, we would all be lost!"

"Bind me tight to the mast. Do not loosen the knots, no matter how I act or what I say, until we are well past," Odysseus ordered. "Make haste!"

The crew did as he bid. They lashed their king to the ship's mast with heavy rope and tied his wrists with a leather thong. Then they blocked their ears with the beeswax and again raised their oars. No man heard even the slap of his blade as it struck the water.

But the ears of Odysseus were open. Beneath the rhythmic splashing he could hear music faint and faraway. At first it sounded like the sea itself, soft as the humming of the waves. But as the ship neared the island, the music grew louder, rising on the wind and rustling the sails. Haunting trills, like those played on a pipe, sounded. A chorus of melodies followed,

sweeter than any from the strings of a lyre. Odysseus leaned forward, the better to listen, straining at the ropes that held him.

The Sirens swam toward the boat. "Come, Odysseus, come!" they coaxed, holding out their arms. The sea nymphs smiled at him, and their eyes, bright and unblinking, glistened like the sun-sparked water. They were so beautiful that Odysseus could not believe the terrible things Circe had said about them.

He struggled to be free. "Loose my bonds!" he demanded.

But the wax in the sailors' ears fit snugly and they could not hear him.

The Sirens encircled the ship and Odysseus could not turn away from their irresistible voices. "Joy! Joy!" they sang. The melody was so exquisite that Odysseus thought his heart would surely burst. Despite the hot sun overhead, he began to shiver.

"Untie me!" he shouted. "Obey your king!"

The sailors rowed on, unhearing and unmindful of both Odysseus and the Sirens.

Now the nymphs tempted Odysseus with words as well as music. "We will give you wisdom," the Sirens promised. "You shall have knowledge of everything now on earth, and of that which is yet to be." Their voices sank to a tantalizing whisper. "Join us in the sea!"

Odysseus was overcome with such longing that he lost his senses. He began to howl, and tears spilled from his eyes. He twisted until the ropes bit at his arms and chest, and he gnawed his lip until blood reddened his beard. Groaning, Odysseus slumped against the mast.

Silently, steadily, the unheeding sailors lifted their oars in and out of the water, pulling the galley past the Island of the Sirens.

The music faded, becoming softer and softer. When Odysseus could no longer distinguish a single note, he raised his head. Looking back, he searched the sea. The nymphs had vanished beneath the waves. But he still could see their island quite clearly. Odysseus stared, horrified, at the splotches of chalky white that stained the gray ledge. Each was a mound, a pile of human bones and skulls. Other men who had listened to the Sirens had not been as fortunate as he. Odysseus's voice rose in a loud lament.

So his men found him, tearstained and bloody, when they came to free him from his bonds. "Set the course," Odysseus commanded wearily. "We sail for Ithaca."

As one, the oarsmen lifted their long paddles. They plunged the blades into the Ionian Sea and the King of Ithaca continued his journey home.

# Hansi and the Nix

$I$f there's water deep enough to splash in, it might be home to a mermaid.

Melusine, the famous French mermaid, was discovered in a woodland spring. In China a fishtailed maiden was found swimming in an urn. Hawaiians have heard mermaids singing in waterfalls, and when the Welsh look into ponds, they sometimes see Lake Ladies herding their mer-cattle.

Germans tell about the Rhine maidens, the sweet-voiced nymphs who haunt that river, while in France dangerous water sprites called *dracs* live in the streams. In Russia the pale-skinned *rusalki* dwell underwater in the winter but move into trees to sing when the weather warms.

Like their saltwater cousins the Sirens, most freshwater mermaids have irresistible voices.

Those humans luckless enough to fall under a mermaid's musical spell seldom see family or friends again. An old Portuguese rhyme warns:

*Danger lurks for him who listens*
*Where the singing mermaid glistens. . . .*

This next folktale, from Switzerland, is unusual, for it tells of a lake maiden who is enchanted by a mortal's song.

*I*n Switzerland, in the Lake of Zug, there once lived a water nymph called a nix.

When the nix was in the lake, she had a tail like any mermaid. When the nix crept onto land, she had legs and feet and toes like any human girl.

The Lake of Zug was the nix's favorite haunt. She liked to look up at the snow-streaked mountains that towered above the lake. She liked to look at the dandelions and daisies that bloomed beside the shore. Best of all, she liked to admire her reflection in the clear water. She inspected herself often, to make certain she wasn't getting wrinkles like a human.

One summer day the nix sat on the shore, combing her hair and singing an old song. She peered into the Lake of Zug and sang,

 *"Go call the Swiss cow,*
 *Go call the Jersey.*
 *They must all come, they must all come,*
 *All come into the barn."*

Suddenly a pebble skipped across the water and a voice added,

*"Hol-de-ree-dee-ah, dee-ah.*
*Hol-de-ree-dee, dee-ah, ho!"*

The nix spun about. Behind her stood a young man, and beside him stood a brown cow. Over her singing, the nix hadn't heard them come. "Stop that!" she scolded. "You're spoiling my song."

"But it's supposed to have a yodel," objected the lad.

"A what?" The nix wondered if a yodel was another kind of cow.

"Hol-de-ree-dee-ah," he sang again, sliding the notes from low to high, up and down the scale. "That's a yodel." He grinned at her. "And I am a cowherd, named Hansi, and my cow is Klara."

The nix smiled back. She did not want to admit that she did not have a name, so she said, "Kindly call me Nixie, and kindly teach me how to yodel."

Hansi left Klara grazing on dandelions and

sat down next to the nix. In no time at all the boy and the water maid discovered that they both liked to eat trout and hated to drink buttermilk. They agreed that cows smell better than goats and that, although yellow was their favorite color, bluebells were their favorite flower. They talked until shadows stretched across the lake and the setting sun had topped each gray mountain with a red nightcap.

"I must return to my village," said Hansi. "Klara will need milking."

"But I don't know how to yodel yet," Nixie protested.

"I shall come back tomorrow and teach you," said Hansi.

"Promise?" asked Nixie.

"I promise," he said.

Then the nix dived into the Lake of Zug, and the last Hansi saw of her was a fishtail splashing where her legs had been.

The next afternoon, when Hansi returned to the lake, he found the nix waiting. She had a beautiful voice, as mermaids do, but yodeling, like whistling, is easy for some and hard for others. "I cannot do it!" wailed Nixie.

"Keep trying," said Hansi, "and I'll be back tomorrow."

Hansi returned the following day, and for all the days of summer. Nixie never tired of trying to yodel, and Hansi never tired of trying to teach her. When Klara tired of dandelions, she found daisies to munch. As autumn came, the chilly alpine air made the nix shiver.

"The water's warm at the bottom of the lake," said Nixie.

"Come home with me and sing by my fire," Hansi offered.

"On land, I'd get old and wrinkled. Then I'd not want to sing at all." She shook her head. "Why don't you come with me instead?"

Hansi looked doubtfully at the lake. He had heard that anyone who followed a mermaid might vanish forever.

"If you're not happy, you can always go home," said Nixie.

"Promise?" asked Hansi.

"I promise," she said.

Hansi held his nose and jumped into the Lake of Zug. Although he sank like a pebble straight to the bottom, he discovered that he could breathe easily. Soon he was wriggling around the lake like a tadpole and playing leapfrog with real frogs.

"Are you happy?" asked the nix.

"As a fish in water," Hansi said, blowing bubbles as proof.

Then one day Nixie found him sitting glumly on a sunken millstone.

"What's wrong?" she asked.

"I'm worried about Klara," Hansi answered, "for it's winter up above. The wind is blowing, the snow is falling, and icicles must be hanging from the roof of the barn."

"Is that all?" Nixie did not want Hansi to leave, so she said, "Wait here and I will fetch your cow for you."

The nix swam to the surface, cracked the ice, and skimmed over the snow and through the village to Hansi's barn. Then she tugged

Klara, bellowing and snorting, down to the bottom of the lake.

"Klara!" Hansi cried. He hugged his cow and fed her tender waterweeds. Then Klara was happy, and so was Hansi.

But when springtime came, Hansi was gloomy again. "It does not seem like spring without wildflowers," he explained.

"Is that all?" asked Nixie. "Wait and I will fetch some for you."

The nix swam to the shore of the Lake of Zug and returned with bluebells and daisies for Hansi and dandelions for Klara.

Then everyone was content. The cow ate, the nix sang, and the cowherd yodeled, the three of them together.

But when the long, warm days of summer came, Hansi looked up through the blue-green water and saw the sun hanging above, as round and yellow as a wheel of cheese.

"The cheese I made from Klara's milk is ripe by now," said Hansi. "Oh, how I would love to taste it!"

"Is that all?" asked Nixie. "Wait and I will get some for you."

Soon ten cheeses as big as grinding stones splashed into the Lake of Zug, and Hansi was happy.

Then Hansi complained that sleeping on the stony lake bed bruised his back, so Nixie brought him his own feather bed. Next he wanted his rocking chair and then his whittling knife and his alpenhorn and his fishing pole. The nix no longer had any time to practice yodeling. She spent most of her days and many of her nights fetching things for Hansi. The more she got for him, the more he needed to be happy.

One evening, before he could ask for anything, Nixie said, "Just you wait, Hansi!" Then she disappeared in the dark water.

Hansi waited. He waited from dusk until midnight, and then, sometime after his tenth yawn, he fell asleep. When he awoke in the morning, he saw the nix perched on the millstone, and spread out around her was his village.

Hansi rubbed his eyes. He counted each shop on every street, and found his own house and barn. All was as he remembered. Sheets flapped on clotheslines, and he could even hear cow bells jangle. The nix had enchanted the town of Zug and brought it down to the bottom of the lake.

"Is that all?" Nixie asked as soon as she saw Hansi.

"That's all." Hansi grinned. "I promise." For now there was nothing left to ask for.

Even today, when the Lake of Zug is calm, you can sometimes see the streets and houses of the town beneath the water. If the air is still, you may hear a mermaid singing:
*"Go call the brown cow,*
*Go call the black one.*
*They must all come, they must all come,*
*All come into the barn."*
And then, like an echo:
*"Hol-de-ree-dee-ah, dee-ah!"*

# And Then the Merman Laughed

Most mermen are as ugly as mermaids are beautiful.

The Irish merman is green toothed, red nosed, and squint eyed. Luckily, he doesn't act as bad as he looks.

In England a mer-wife keeps a close eye on her greedy mer-husband or else he might devour their mer-children for tea.

Just catching sight of a merman in China is an ill omen. The fishtailed Ocean Men come to the surface only during storms.

The *vodyanik*, a bearded and bloodthirsty Russian merman, is half man and half frog. He's been known to disguise himself as a harmless floating log.

In Scandinavian lore the water men are usually friendlier. The Danish *havmand*, a handsome fellow, is an ocean-going merman, while a *neck* can be heard in a freshwater river as he strums songs on his harp. Norwegian fishermen hope to catch a *marmel*, the thumb-size merman that brings good luck.

Male or female, ugly or beautiful, most merfolk are thought to be wise. They know which herbs will cure an illness and where riches lie hidden, and they can foresee the future. When one of these water people is captured by a human, it is seldom freed without sharing a secret or promising a reward.

In this story from Iceland the merman may not be good-looking, but he sees the unseen and knows the unknown.

*S*ome years after the Vikings first steered their dragon-headed boats across the sea to Iceland, a Norseman named Tor landed on that island. Tor came to seek his fortune. His wife, Gudrin, came too, to make sure he found it.

Tor tried his hand at farming. But his hay withered in the field and his turnips were freckled with black spots.

Tor kept a milk cow, but he did not keep her long. She bawled, she kicked, and then she ran off and got lost in a bog.

Arctic foxes ate Tor's ducklings, and his whole flock of sheep played follow-the-leader off the edge of a cliff.

All Tor had left was his dog. "A sheepdog without sheep is good for nothing," Tor said sadly.

"Then the dog is just like his master," snapped Gudrin.

"What can I do?" Tor whined.

"Fish!" Gudrin replied. "You'll not be any worse at fishing than at anything else."

Tor was no better at fishing, either. If he baited his lines for large fish, the ocean swarmed with small herring. If he gathered his nets to catch herring, the water jumped with cod and salmon.

On a certain trip, Tor wandered beyond his usual fishing ground. He steered his skiff into the windblown sea and rowed until he reached a distant bank. These waters were strange and mysterious, and even the familiar mountains with their white wigs of snow were lost in the mist.

Tor moored his boat beside a rocky islet. For two days he caught no fish. When Tor cast his line on the third morning, something powerful snatched it and tugged so hard that he almost pitched headfirst from the boat.

Tor braced his foot against the oarlock and heaved. The creature jerked and thrashed, but the line held fast. "I shall take you yet, you sea monster!" Tor shouted.

Suddenly the line went slack in Tor's hands. As he pulled it in, he soon saw that his catch had not swallowed the bait and the barb. Instead, the hook had snagged its tail.

Carefully Tor hauled it up.

"By thunder!" he exclaimed.

Flopping on the bottom of his boat was something with the smooth, sleek tail of a seal. Seaweed trailed from its fins, and barnacles clung to its ears. But this was no sea monster. It was surprisingly small, and from its waist to the top of its bushy-haired head it seemed almost as human as Tor himself.

"Is it—are you—a merman?" Tor asked.

The man-seal glared at Tor with eyes as cold as glacial ice.

Tor's scalp prickled. He wanted to throw the merman back and paddle away as fast as he could. But the barb had torn his tail, and Tor could not ignore any injured living thing.

Gently he pulled out the hook. "I shall take you home until you're healed," said Tor.

The merman whistled between his teeth and did not answer.

At first the return journey was easy, for the wind was light and the water calm. Then, without warning, a squall blew up. The sky above

was blue, but the sea beneath Tor's boat was black and churning like a whirlpool. Huge waves battered the skiff, half filling it with water. He was certain the creature had whistled up the storm. Tor clung to the anchor and cried, "Heaven help us."

Drenched and exhausted, they reached the shore at last. The merman, slung over Tor's shoulder, felt as heavy as a sack of sand. Tor's sheepdog growled at the merman in greeting.

"Good-for-nothing!" grumbled Tor, pushing the dog away.

And then the merman laughed.

Tor jumped and almost dropped him. "Why do you laugh?" he asked, but got no answer.

As Tor crossed the field to his house, he stumbled over a tussock. "Worthless weed!" He stamped the wiry grass.

And then the merman laughed again.

This time Tor almost dropped the merman on purpose. "Why?" he questioned, but still got no reply.

Gudrin watched Tor coming, hunched

beneath his burden. "What's that you carry?" she called.

"See for yourself," Tor replied.

Curious, Gudrin came closer. "Ugh!" she cried. "What a slimy tail! What an ugly face! *What is it?*"

Tor put his finger to his lips. The man-seal did not speak, but surely he heard. "He is a merman. Perhaps he brings luck."

"Bad luck!" his wife complained. "A sea dwarf! That's the reward you bring me for all my hard work and sweet nature."

Tor looked down at his boots. "I'm sorry—" he began, but his words were drowned out. The merman was looking at Gudrin and laughing for the third time, long and loud.

Gudrin scowled. "You'll not bring that animal inside."

Tor quickly consented, for their sod house, built into the hillside, had only one room. He put the merman in the stable instead.

Each morning Tor brought the merman his fair share of bread and salted herring. He often stayed to talk, but it was always Tor who did the speaking, and the merman the listening. Two weeks passed in this way before the merman's tail was fully healed.

"Now we can sell that sea thing at the market in Volgar," Gudrin said. She looked slyly at the merman. "Perhaps he will please somebody—for supper!"

This upset Tor almost as much as it did the merman. When Gudrin left, Tor told the manseal, "Pay her no heed. I will return you to the ocean, if first you teach me the charms merfolk know."

Then the merman spoke in a voice squeaky and rusty from disuse: "Magic is a gift. It cannot be taught."

Tor sighed. "At least you can tell me why you laughed."

"Take me to the fishing bank where I was caught; then you shall hear," the merman promised.

The next day, before the sun had melted the mist or Gudrin had opened her eyes, Tor set off with the merman. The sea was calm and they reached the rocky islet quickly. The merman grasped the oar blade, ready to dive into the sea.

"Not yet!" Tor pleaded. "Tell me why you laughed the first time."

"Because you drove away your dog," the merman answered, "while, in all the world, he's the most faithful to you."

"Why did you laugh the second time?"

"Because you seek a fortune," said the merman, "while there's buried treasure for the taking under the tussock you kicked."

Tor's eyes widened. "And the third time you laughed?"

"Because you trust your wife while that unfaithful woman gossips and complains behind your back." The merman chuckled. "Nothing escapes my ears."

Saying no more, the merman plunged into the sea.

Tor lost little time in rowing home. Although he could not prove his dog's loyalty, nor his wife's disloyalty, he could look beneath the tussock.

Tor yanked out the mound of grass and dug buckets of dirt, but he found only a beetle or two. "The merman tricked me," he grumbled, throwing down his shovel.

The blade rang against metal. Excited, Tor dug frantically with his hands until he uncovered a small iron chest. When he pried open the lid, a shower of golden coins fell out.

"Treasure from a Viking raider!" Clutching his booty, Tor hurried home.

"A gift from the man-seal," Tor told his astonished wife. "The merman knows all and hears all. And he laughs at all who are foolish."

Gudrin's cheeks turned red, but she dared not say a word, then or later. For she never knew when the merman might be listening.

As for Tor, wherever he fished, on any day, his nets were always full. And then it was Tor who laughed.

# The Listening Ear

Mermaids are shape-shifters. In the blink of an eye, a mermaid may become someone—or something—quite different.

In both Asia and Europe mermaids put on the feathers of swans. On the Isle of Man mermaids escape capture by changing into wrens, while mermen in Caribbean waters are said to sneak ashore as cats.

On some South Pacific islands it is still forbidden—*tabu*—to catch a dolphin, for it could be a mermaid in disguise. In Ireland mermaids are able to turn into harmless, hornless little cows, or become gentle seals called the *roane*. When Scottish merfolk slip into their gray sealskins, they become *selkies*.

In Scotland a merman may also transform himself into a water horse called a *kelpie*. Kelpies are full-size stallions, handsome but savage. A human foolish enough to mount a kelpie is stuck to its back like a barnacle to a rock. Then the horse plunges into the water, drowning its unlucky rider.

Many mermaids, already half fish, become full fish. Salmon and trout are likely choices. But in this *mukashibanashi*, or fairy tale, from Japan, the mermaid changes from a slippery snapper to a quivery jellyfish.

*I*n old Japan, on the shores of the Inland Sea, there once lived a lad named Jiro. Jiro was a second son. As was the custom then, his older brother, Taro, the firstborn son, got first chance and first choice in everything.

If there was only one meat dumpling, Taro ate it, and Jiro had yesterday's rice.

If not enough coins rattled in the money jar to pay for both boys' schooling, it was Taro who went to lessons and Jiro who stayed behind.

Since the two were friends as well as brothers, Jiro did not complain. "I take whatever comes my way," he said cheerfully.

One day, when the sun was high and the tide was low, Jiro waded along the seashore, searching for treasures left behind by the waves. Early that same morning, at the Hour of the Hare, he'd fished a fine straw hat from the water, as good as new. Now he found nothing at all. Jiro had turned to go home when he spied something red splashing in a tidepool.

"Lucky me!" he cried. "It's a snapper. A red *tai*."

In such shallow water the snapper was as helpless as a goldfish in a teacup. Jiro scooped it up in his straw hat. "Tonight Taro and I shall both eat fish cake," he said.

The snapper gazed up at him with glassy eyes and gasped as if it were sobbing. Jiro stared back. All of a sudden, he swung his hat and flipped the fish into the ocean. "A light heart's better than a full stomach," Jiro declared.

He'd taken but a few steps down the beach when a voice called, "Please wait!"

Jiro spun around. Ankle deep in sea foam stood a beautiful, pale-cheeked maiden. The silk of her kimono was the rosy red of the sky at twilight.

"Surely you do not call me," said Jiro.

"I call the one who spared my life," the maiden replied.

Jiro was puzzled, but he bowed politely to show respect. As he bent his head, he saw the tip of a fishtail beneath her kimono. "You are a *ningyo*!" he gasped. "A mermaid!"

"I am Tamayori, daughter of Rin Jin the Dragon King who rules the ocean." She smiled at Jiro. "But you met me first in a different form."

Jiro blinked. The shiny red of her kimono seemed familiar. "The snapper!" he blurted.

"My father will wish to thank you for your kindness," said the sea maiden, beckoning. "Come with me."

"I do not swim," Jiro protested.

"I shall become a jellyfish and you can ride on my back."

The maiden sank beneath the froth. Bubbles rose to the surface, and in her place floated a large jellyfish.

"Well," said Jiro, straddling the slippery creature, "I take whatever comes my way." He clapped his hat to his head with one hand, held tight to a tentacle with the other, and squeezed his eyes shut.

The jellyfish drifted down, down, down beneath the waves. Strangely, Jiro could breathe in the salty water without swallowing a mouthful. When the jellyfish slid to a stop on the ocean floor, Jiro opened his eyes and looked about.

Crabs scuttled sideways through the sea grass, and orange and purple starfish stretched their arms out in the sand. The water above was as blue as the summer sky, and a thousand colored fish swam in it like bright-feathered birds. Beside him stood Tamayori, once more in her maiden form.

"Welcome to the kingdom of Neriya," she said. "Come."

Bobbing as lightly as a sponge, Jiro followed her through the underwater world until they reached a magnificent palace. The tall pillars were carved from coral, and the roof was tiled with pearls. An octopus guarded the arched gateway.

"This is Jiro-san of Japan," Tamayori told the octopus. To Jiro she said, "My father awaits you in the Great Hall."

The Great Hall was a vast sea cavern, lighted

by lanterns made from blowfish. Sprawled on a throne in the center was an enormous beast. A scaly tail thrust from beneath its robe, its hands were claws, and the hair on its chin and its head was spiky green seaweed. Jiro was sure that this was Rin Jin the Dragon King, and he knelt to hide his shaking knees.

The Dragon King smiled, showing rows of teeth as sharp as a shark's. "My daughter is dearer to me than anything else in the sea," he explained to Jiro. "I shall reward you well for saving her life. Whatever your heart desires shall be yours."

"Most honorable one . . ." Jiro began. He hesitated, his mind spinning with visions of chests overflowing with jewels and heaping piles of gleaming silver and gold.

"Ask for the Listening Ear," Tamayori hissed.

"I have two good ears," Jiro whispered back. "They work together very well and fit quite nicely on my head. What need have I of another?"

The sea maiden's smile vanished. Her dark brows drew together in an angry scowl, and she flushed as red as when she was a *tai*. Alarmed, Jiro said loudly, "If you please, Your Highness, I . . . I choose the Listening Ear."

The Dragon King sprang up. "No!" he roared. "Never!" He thrashed his tail, shaking the Great Hall like an earthquake. Pointing a claw at Jiro, Rin Jin demanded, "How does a common creature such as yourself know of the Listening Ear?"

Jiro looked down at the sandy floor. "I just recently learned of it."

The furious Dragon King turned to his daughter. "Did you dare reveal . . . ?"

Tamayori did not drop her eyes but steadily returned his gaze. "You promised Jiro his heart's desire, my father."

"Aaagh!" Rin Jin moaned as if in pain. "Must I give this ordinary boy my most extra-ordinary treasure?"

Tamayori nodded. "A rightful reward for my life."

The Great Hall fell silent. It was so still that Jiro could hear a clam open up its shell to listen. At last Rin Jin signaled the octopus. "The King of Neriya will keep his word," he said.

The octopus slithered behind a rock and crept out with two of his eight arms clasped about a plain red box. Then the Dragon King bellowed at Jiro, *"Take it!"*

Jiro snatched the box and backed, bowing, from the hall. He plunged through the sea grass while Tamayori floated quietly at his side. When they reached the gate, Jiro turned to her and said, "I must go, Princess Tamayori. My brother, Taro, expects me at home."

"Stay!" she begged. "My father's anger will not last long. It is like a passing squall, not a typhoon." Tamayori caught his hand. "We will celebrate with seaweed soup, with oysters and lobsters."

Jiro's mouth watered, but he shook his head. "I cannot remain. It is beside the sea that I belong, not in it."

Tamayori dropped Jiro's hand. Without

another word, she again became a jellyfish and carried him swiftly to the shore. Then, in a swirl of waves, the mermaid disappeared.

Jiro climbed the sandy bank and squinted up at the sky. It was midday, the Hour of the Horse, and the sun was still high. His visit to the kingdom of Neriya had taken no time at all. He would have thought it all a daydream if it had not been for the box in his hand. Slowly Jiro raised the lid. Inside lay a yellowed, chipped conch shell.

"Oya!" he groaned. "So this is the Listening Ear! All that uproar was over a broken seashell!"

Jiro's eyes smarted as he thought of all the riches he might have asked for in its place. Then he shrugged. "So? I take whatever comes my way," he said. "At least I can listen to the ocean and remember my strange adventure."

He held the shell up to his ear. But the sounds Jiro heard were not from the sea. Instead, he listened to gulls quarreling overhead and a flock of sparrows gossiping in a pine tree. He heard far more than their squawks and chirps. With the conch shell pressed against his ear, Jiro knew what they were saying. He understood the language of the birds!

Jiro caught his breath in wonder, turned toward the ocean, and cupped his hands. "Ten thousand thanks, Tamayori," he shouted, "for the Listening Ear!"

In some cherry trees nearby, three crows were chattering. Jiro listened, holding the shell like an ear trumpet.

"Kaa! Kaa!" cawed the first crow. "Medicine cannot cure the nobleman's daughter."

"Can't! Can't!" jeered a second. "Osada is under the spell of the hungry snake that is trapped in the roof."

"Foolish humans!" scolded a third. "They need only to free the snake and feed it, and Osada would soon be well."

Jiro had not heard of Osada's illness, but he had often heard of her kindness to others. He slipped the shell into its box and took off at a trot for the nobleman's house. Although it was not far from his home, he had never dared to venture there before. A signboard swung on the iron gate.

REWARD TO THE ONE WHO CURES OSADA

Jiro struck the brass gong and called boldly, "Hear this! I have come to cure Osada."

The nobleman's servants peeked at Jiro through the bars of the gate. He was barefoot, and salt water dropped from his straw hat. "The fellow smells like fish," they said, holding their noses.

The nobleman's doctors inspected Jiro from a distance and turned their backs. "That bundle of rags can never cure Osada."

But the nobleman himself, most anxious about his daughter, unlocked the gate and declared, "Let the boy try."

Osada lay on a futon. Her eyes were open but unseeing, and a full dish of rice sat untouched beside her.

Jiro took off his hat and shook his head.

"Some creature suffers. That is the cause of this worthy lady's illness." He pointed at the roof. "A snake is trapped in the thatch."

The servants smirked and slapped their knees and the doctors laughed aloud, but the nobleman ordered, "Off with the roof!"

At once, a dozen workmen ripped at the roof with long-handled axes. As clumps of thatch tumbled to the floor, an enormous snake, half dead from hunger, slithered slowly down a beam.

Osada fluttered her eyelids.

Jiro reached for the bowl of rice and put it before the serpent.

The snake's tongue darted into the bowl. Osada turned her head and smiled at her father and Jiro.

The snake swallowed a mouthful. Osada pushed herself up from her mat.

When the snake had eaten the last grain of rice, it swished out the door. Osada skipped across the room to her father.

"My daughter is dearer to me than anything

else on earth," the nobleman told Jiro. "How can I reward you for saving her life?"

Jiro bowed to Osada. "Her recovery is my reward," he said.

Osada blushed. "Stay!" she begged. "We shall celebrate with melons and peaches and sweet stuffed plums."

Jiro swallowed hard before he answered. "I must go. My brother, Taro, expects me at home."

"You shall not leave empty-handed," the nobleman declared. "Hold out your hat."

Jiro did so. The nobleman ordered servants to fill the straw hat to the brim with gold *ryo* coins. Jiro bowed low and then started toward the door.

"Is there no way for me to show my gratitude?" Osada asked.

"You may, noble lady," Jiro murmured, "by allowing me to visit you again."

Taro was waiting when Jiro got home. "What kept you?" asked the older brother. "It is already the Hour of the Dog, and I have already eaten the bean cakes."

"Something better than bean cakes came my way today," said Jiro. He emptied his hatful of money on the table and told of all the strange and wonderful things that had happened to him. Taro listened openmouthed, gaping first at the pile of golden coins and then at his younger brother.

"When I met the mermaid, my luck began," Jiro declared. "But when I wed the kind Osada, I shall be luckier still."

"You will wed Osada?" Taro scratched his head. "How can you be so certain?"

"I know what's going to come my way." Smiling, Jiro held up the Listening Ear. "A bird told me."

Outside in the courtyard, a nightingale sang.

# The Sea Princess
# and the Sea Witch

Not so very long ago, many sailors in many parts of the world believed that mermaids were water witches.

European seamen blamed mermaids for stirring up gales, and thought they could make the ocean boil and cook the fish.

In the West Indies sailors accused mermaids of trying to steal men's shadows. If one succeeded, the man was bewitched forever.

Brazilian fishermen prayed to Iemanja, the African goddess of the sea, for safekeeping from mermaids.

Some sailors tried to bribe a mermaid by tossing gold coins or treasures into an angry sea. Mediterranean fishermen hoped to please her by pouring a glass of wine into the water.

Other seamen tried instead to scare any mermaids away. In times past, those who sailed the Atlantic threw their daggers overboard. Anything made with iron was a charm against witches, so they hoped to make mermaids dive and disappear. For personal protection a sailor might sew a "witches' bag" inside his jacket. The pouch was stuffed with guts of toad or liver of hare to ward off mermaids.

But there's no defense against some water witches, like the one in this story from the Hebrides Islands of Scotland.

Once, when the coastal waters off Scotland held as much magic as salt, there was a sea princess. The King of the Sea was her father, the queen was her mother, and they lived in a grand sand castle at the bottom of the ocean.

The princess was different from her parents. When they were in the water, the king and queen had graceful fishtails. Not so their daughter. She always had two feet and ten toes.

"Toes are ugly," the princess complained to her mother. "Tails are better for swimming. Will I ever grow one?"

"No." The queen shook her head. "You take after your great-grandfather." She added kindly, "A most handsome sailor."

"A *human*?" cried the princess. "Did you really see him?"

"Once, long ago, on the island of Staffa, when I went there to gather apples."

"Take me to visit Staffa," begged the princess.

"You are too young," replied the queen, "and it is too dangerous."

Each autumn, the queen went by herself to visit the deserted island of Staffa. She liked to roam the rocky beach that stretched beneath the gray bluffs. She took care not to wander near the cave where the yellow sea grapes grew on their sickly green stems, for that was the lair of the sea witch. The witch was said to know all the secrets of the sea, but the queen did not trust her to use her skills for good.

The queen walked in the opposite direction, searching for wave-tossed treasures and looking for windfalls that dropped from a cliff-top apple tree. The tree, although old and gnarled, bore sweet rosy fruit. The queen always saved the biggest and reddest apple for her daughter.

"Remember," the queen would caution as the princess bit into the apple, "not everything on land is good to eat!"

On one of the queen's visits to Staffa, a great storm arose. Before she could reach the safety of deep water, wild sea horses rushed from the ocean and galloped over the rocks. The queen, caught in their path, died beneath their hooves.

The Sea King locked himself in his chambers, mourning her for a year and a day. When at last he ventured out, he saw his daughter, silent and sad, her brown eyes clouded with tears.

"How selfish I have been," cried the king. "You are even more in want of a mother than I am of a wife."

Then the King of the Sea himself visited the island of Staffa. He went to the cave where the yellow sea grapes grew on their sickly green stems. "Wisewoman!" he called. "You are the keeper of knowledge. Tell me where to find a mother for my daughter."

"Here, my lord." The sea witch came out of the cave. She was beautiful, with hair as black as a sea raven's wings and eyes the gray-green of the ocean. "Take me as wife. When I am queen, I will care for the princess."

So the king married the sea witch and took her to his pearly-white palace beneath the ocean. The witch put on the queen's robes and sat on the queen's throne. She wore the queen's jewels and slept in the queen's bed. But she did not care for the queen's daughter.

Each day the witch invented a terrible task for the princess. "Sweep the sand from the ocean floor," she demanded, or, "Count every herring in the sea!"

The king, busy managing the currents and the tides, paid little attention to matters in the palace. Still, despite her father's absentminded neglect and the witch's intended cruelty, the natural beauty of the princess grew with the years.

One evening the king put aside his time-tables and sea charts and inspected the princess. "You have done well," he praised the witch. "My daughter is the fairest in the ocean!"

Envy, bitter and burning, rose in the sea witch's throat. "I am not yet finished with her," she replied.

The next day the witch told the princess, "A special task awaits us on Staffa."

The princess was overjoyed to visit the island at last. But once there, she grew wistful for her mother. "Have we come for apples?" she asked.

"Apples? Bah!" spat the witch. "I've something better in mind."

She led the princess to the cave where the yellow sea grapes grew. "Try one," she urged.

The princess picked a grape. But she remembered her mother's warning and did not eat it. The witch pinched the girl's cheeks and pushed the grape into her open mouth. "Swallow!" she screeched.

The princess choked and the grape rolled down her throat. At once she felt whiskers sprouting on her cheeks. Her arms numbed and became flippers. Her legs began to tingle, and a tail grew where her feet had been.

The sea witch smirked. "You wanted a tail!"

The princess looked at her reflection in a tidepool. Her own brown eyes stared back from the face of a seal.

"A seal you are and a seal you shall stay," the

witch chanted in her ear, "save for one night and one day each year. Then, when the harvest moon shines bright above Staffa, you may again become a princess."

The sea witch left the seal maiden by the cave. "Now who's the fairest in the ocean?" called the witch, and she chuckled all the way back to the Sea King's palace.

"Your nuisance of a daughter is gone," she told him.

"Gone where?" asked the king, bewildered.

"Gone and lost forever," the witch answered. "And good riddance, say I."

"Evil one!" thundered the king. "This is your wicked doing! It is *you* who shall be gone . . . now!"

The king never saw the sea witch again. And he never knew that the shy seal that swam beside the palace was the princess.

Once every twelve months, when the apples were ripe and the moon was full, a seal climbed out of the sea and onto Staffa's stony beach.

Slipping from the sealskin, it became a maiden and remained so until sundown the next day. One such time, when the princess was wandering the beach, she saw a young fisherman sitting on the flat rock.

"You're a human!" she exclaimed.

The lad gawked at her. "As human as you are."

The girl laughed and stared down at her feet. "We are a lot alike."

"I'm not nearly so pretty," the fisherlad replied.

The princess smiled. "Please stay," she said, "just for today."

The lad caught hold of her hand. Together they gathered apples, looked for seashells, and danced in the waves to the music of the sea. But as the sun disappeared into the ocean, the maiden suddenly broke away and vanished into the shadows.

"Come back!" called the fisherlad.

He scrambled after her but found only a small gray seal, gazing up at him with warm brown eyes. Then the fisherlad understood. This was no ordinary girl. She was a *selkie*—a seal maiden.

Every autumn, until he was an old, old man, the fisherman came back to Staffa. He never married, nor loved another. He sat on the same rock, a ripe apple in his hand, knowing that his sea princess would return.

# Pania of the Reef

Wherever they live in the world's waters, mermaids have a lot in common.

Few of them can stay ashore for long. Most cannot bear the bright sunlight, and drown in the air like fish out of water. Those who are able to settle on land still miss the sea. Even when kept in a pool, a mermaid so yearns for open water that she often pales and withers away.

Sound-alike mermaid tales are told on opposite sides of the globe. In a Scottish story, a lad steals a mermaid's seal hide to keep her from returning to the ocean. In the Solomon Islands of the South Pacific, a boy snatches a sea maiden's dolphin skin for the same reason. In time, both maidens recover their magical animal coats and escape to their underwater homes.

The mermaid in this Maori tale comes from

New Zealand, in the southern hemisphere. But she has story cousins on the other side of the equator. Like "Mrs. Fitzgerald the Merrow," she marries a mortal and lives ashore. Like the sea maiden in the Japanese story "The Listening Ear," she is a shape-shifter. Sometimes this Maori mermaid is linked to storyteller Hans Christian Andersen's famous "The Little Mermaid," for both mermaids are betrayed by the humans they love.

Matching one mermaid tale with another isn't hard. What's difficult is trying to match a mermaid with a mortal man.

$\mathcal{W}$ithout a splash, Pania skimmed over the reef. Without a ripple, she swam to the foot of Hukarere Cliff. There, where a freshwater stream runs into the bay, she hid among the flax bushes. Without a sound, she waited.

Pania did so each evening, as soon as the sun had cooled its fire in the ocean. For when daylight faded to dusk, she knew he would come.

He was Kari-toki, son of the chief in the nearby *pa*, or village. Kari-toki was a warrior, long-legged and wide-shouldered, with tattoos scattered across his cheekbones like a constellation of stars. Never before had Pania seen so handsome a man. It was for love of Kari-toki that she left her home in the sea each evening.

Kari-toki came to the spring at the foot of Hukarere Cliff to quench his thirst. The water here tasted especially sweet, well worth the steep walk down the slippery path. Kari-toki filled his gourd cup again and again, not knowing that someone was watching him.

Many weeks passed in this way, and at last Pania could keep her silence no longer. Late one afternoon, after Kari-toki had drained the last drop of water from the gourd and was about to return to his village, Pania murmured an ancient charm:

*"Aroha mai, aroha atu."* Love given needs love returned.

Pania's voice was no louder than the breeze rustling the stiff flax, yet her whispered spell reached Kari-toki's ears.

"Who are you?" he cried, wheeling around. "Where are you?"

"I am Pania," she answered, and stepped from her hiding place.

Kari-toki caught his breath. She who called herself Pania was not of his village. She was not a *ponaturi* either, for those ghostly ocean fairies had skin as white as cockleshells. Pania's skin was the glossy brown of a cowrie shell, and when she looked at him her dark eyes shone.

No human woman was ever so beautiful. Whoever Pania might be, Kari-toki loved her at once.

"Be my wife," he said, holding out his hand. "For I will marry you and no other."

Pania smiled, pleased with the strong magic of the charm. "Be my husband," she replied.

Holding each other's hands, they pledged their love. And so, by Maori custom, they were married.

Pania followed Kari-toki up to the top of the cliff and through a forest of totara trees to his village. In the darkness, none of the villagers saw her enter Kari-toki's *whare*, or hut. She remained at his side throughout the night, but as soon as *kopu*, the morning star, moved across the sky, Pania arose.

Kari-toki's eyes were still heavy with sleep. "Why do you go?" he mumbled.

"I must leave the world of light," Pania answered, "and return to the shadows of the sea."

Now wide awake, Kari-toki sat up. "But you are my wife!" he protested.

"So I am," said Pania, "and so I will meet you by Hukarere Cliff after sundown tonight, and for all the nights to come."

She slipped out the door and hurried down the forest path before others in the village even stirred.

Pania was true to her word. Each twilight she waited for Kari-toki, but she no longer hid among the flax. Instead she spent her time diving for crayfish and prying off the mussels that clung to the reef. She gave these gifts from the sea to her husband, and sometimes she had pieces of shiny jade greenstone to offer him as well.

Pania always came to the village after dark, and she always left before dawn. Although Kari-toki often boasted of Pania and her beauty, no one else had ever seen her.

"Your wife disappears in the morning like a dream," said a friend.

"Perhaps Kari-toki is having a nightmare and mistakes a piece of driftwood for a wife," another joked.

Kari-toki scowled, wishing he could delay Pania's leaving long enough for others to gaze at her. Then, suddenly, he had an idea.

"Tomorrow you will see Pania for yourselves," he declared.

All day, Kari-toki hauled pots of wet clay to his hut. He sealed even the smallest cracks in the walls with the mud, shutting out the sun. When he had finished, the inside of his *whare* was as dark as a cave.

That night Pania joined Kari-toki as usual. He had prepared a feast of mutton-bird and sweet potato, but she shook her head.

"Food from the land does not suit me," she said, and nibbled on the raw fish she had brought with her.

Kari-toki did not argue but ate his own food. Then, with both their stomachs full, they fell asleep.

Pania awoke first and turned to Kari-toki. "It must be morning," she said. "I hear the waves calling me."

"It is night," he answered. "See how dark it is."

Since that was so, Pania put her head down again. But soon she heard the cry of a bird.

"The bell bird is singing to *ra*, the sun," she exclaimed.

"It is still night," answered Kari-toki, "and you hear *ruru*, the owl, talking to himself."

As Pania lay down once more, she saw a sliver of sunlight creep under the door. "It *is* day!" she cried. "You have fooled me!"

Pania ran outside, into the shade of the forest, down the steep cliff, and splashed into the cool of the sea. And except for Kari-toki, no one in the village gazed upon her that day, or any other.

Kari-toki did not try to trick Pania again. A year passed, and in the next a fine baby boy was born to them. Since he was bald like most babies, they called him Moremore: "One-with-no-hair." Kari-toki wished to keep the boy at home, but Pania took him with her each morning.

"He, too, is a creature of the sea," she said.

Now Kari-toki spent much time in thought. He wanted Moremore to belong to the land as well. Most of all he wanted his father, the chief, to see his splendid grandson and to choose a fitting name for him. But no idea came to Kari-toki this time. At last he went to the *tohunga* — the village wise man — for advice.

The *tohunga* believed Kari-toki when he spoke of Pania, for he knew of ocean maidens. He knew, too, what Kari-toki must do to keep Pania and the baby with him.

"One who swallows cooked food cannot live in the sea," said the *tohunga*.

"But Pania will not eat human food," said Kari-toki.

"When she sleeps," said the *tohunga*, "slip a morsel into her mouth. Then give a bit to One-with-no-hair to chew upon."

Kari-toki did as the wise man said. That very day he stewed a pot of taro and hid it beneath a basket in a corner.

When Pania came into the hut that evening, she sniffed and wrinkled her nose. "Ugh! Something smells terrible!" she said. But she did not ask what it was, nor did she search to find out for herself.

That night Kari-toki watched as Pania slept, counting each breath until he was sure she would not wake. Then he tiptoed to the pot of taro and took two small pieces. One he placed in the corner of Pania's mouth. As he was about to give the other to Moremore, the baby looked up at him and laughed.

"Shhhh!" cautioned Kari-toki.

His warning came too late. Moremore's laugh woke Pania. She sat up, and the bit of taro fell from her mouth.

"How could you?" Pania cried. She guessed at once what Kari-toki was up to. Snatching Moremore, she fled from the hut.

Kari-toki stumbled after them. The totara trees hid the moon, and he tripped over roots and slipped on pebbles. When he reached the top of Hukarere Cliff, he saw a shadow standing in the spray far below. "Pania!" shouted Kari-toki. "Wait!"

Pania looked up at him. "If you had loved me enough, this would not have happened," she said.

Kari-toki started down the bluff. "This has happened because I loved you *too* much," he protested.

Pania sighed, but she waded farther from shore. When the water reached her shoulders, she hugged her baby, bent, and gave him to the ocean. At once, One-with-no-hair kicked his heels and swam away. He had changed into *mango*, the shark.

Pania turned toward Kari-toki and held out her arms. Then she herself sank into the water that swirled around the reef.

Kari-toki plunged after her, but found only a rock marking the place where she had been. Pania had returned to the sea and to her people.

*The rock still stands by the reef in Hawke Bay on the North Island of New Zealand. It is almost human in shape. Eels and snappers swim beneath the outstretched arms, and crayfish hide at the base. Often a small, smooth reef shark is seen circling around it.*

*Like the statue of Andersen's Little Mermaid in Copenhagen, Denmark, a bronze likeness of Pania stands in Napier, New Zealand. Called Pania of the Reef, she waits without a sound among the flax.*

# Notes on the Stories

## Mrs. Fitzgerald the Merrow

Liban the Mermaid, first of the Irish merrows, appeared in the nine-hundred-year-old *Book of the Dun Cow*. Although not so ancient, the story of "Mrs. Fitzgerald the Merrow" has been known for at least two centuries. This retelling is based on "The Lady of Gollerus" from *Fairy Legends and Traditions of the South of Ireland* by T. Crofton Croker (London: John Murray, Ltd., 1825).

## The Legend of Aymee and the Mermaid

Until recently, traditional Alaskan stories were

heard, not read, for none of the twenty native languages was written down until after the coming of the Russians in the eighteenth century. Lela Kiana Oman recalled listening to "Aymee and the Mermaid" as a child in her village *gasgich*, or community hall. The tale is from her collection *Eskimo Legends* (Anchorage: Alaska Methodist University Press, 1975).

## Odysseus and the Sirens

Some early accounts said that the Sirens had the heads of beautiful women and the bodies of birds. Later writers gave them fishtails. Homer left the specifics of a Siren's appearance to the reader's imagination, for these tempters aren't described in *The Odyssey*, the account of Odysseus's travels. This interpretation is based on Albert Cook's translation (New York: W. W. Norton & Company, Inc., 1967).

## Hansi and the Nix

One night in 1435, two streets in the village of Zug suddenly sank into Lake Zug. Scholars claimed that the water had undermined the land, but others said that a nix must be to blame. "Hansi and the Nix" is adapted from *Water Spirits*, in the Enchanted World series (Alexandria, Va.: Time-Life Books, 1985). "Calling the Cows" is a Swiss folk song.

## And Then the Merman Laughed

In Iceland, even today, if someone says something especially foolish, a listener may comment, "And then the merman laughed." That adage comes from this story. My retelling relies on the version in *Icelandic Folktales and Legends* by Jacqueline Simpson (Berkeley, Calif.: University of California Press, 1972).

# The Listening Ear

The ability to understand the language of animals is a theme repeated in folklore throughout the world. In Japan there are at least fourteen variations of this particular story. My adaptation is based on "The Magic Ear" from *Folktales of Japan* by the respected story collector Keigo Seki (Chicago: University of Chicago Press, 1963).

## The Sea Princess and the Sea Witch

Lore from the Hebrides (or Western) Islands, off the coast of Scotland, dates back to the time of the Druids. Staffa, an uninhabited inner island, is the most likely locale for "The Sea Princess and the Sea Witch" because of its distinctive cave formations. This retelling is based upon "The Seal Maiden" from *Folklore of All*

*Nations* by F. H. Lee (New York: Tudor Publishing Company, 1930).

## Pania of the Reef

The Maori of New Zealand are Polynesians, kin to Tahitians and other Pacific peoples. Many of these islanders share similar ocean stories, and almost all their supernatural sea beings share Pania's horror of sunlight. This story closely follows the tale "Pania," found in the *Treasury of Maori Folklore* by Alexander W. Reed (Wellington, New Zealand: A. H. and A. W. Reed, 1963).